Lost in the Forest

A Romantic Wilderness Adventure

Anna Leigh

DEDICATION

For Tara Lynn Caton, a free spirit who touched so many lives and left this earth too soon. You are missed.

ACKNOWLEDGMENTS

No book can be completed without the help of many others, usually too numerous to mention all by name. Here are a few, and forgive me if I have excluded someone – I would write someone important, but you are all important to me.

First, my family, without who's encouragement, this would have not been completed. Especially my mom, who always thought this would be done. Next, my proofreader, Sally Garst for her efforts to correct my errant ways. Then, to the group of reviewers who provided valuable insight and impetus for changing this work in ways to make it better. Finally, to Gundi Gabrielle and the SassyZenGirl network for their assistance.

Cover by Lizaa

One

The four-year-old Toyota Corolla turned off the two-lane asphalt road and into the parking lot. Holly Franklin, behind the wheel, heard the crunch of gravel beneath the tires. She pulled to the creosote impregnated log that served as the parking boundary, put the car into 'park,' and turned off the engine. She sat looking at the scene before her. The sun was shining on a meadow. Behind that, aspen trees with yellow-gold leaves were interspersed with the dark green fir trees. In the distance were majestic peaks dusted with snow.

Holly smiled. She'd been given a gift of a day off during the work week. They didn't come often. And this one came with perfect autumn weather. She'd left her place in Denver early and drove first to Estes Park, then to a parking area at the start of a hiking trail – a loop – that would take about four hours, more or less, to complete. Even at four hours, she calculated, she would be back home by mid- to late afternoon.

Holly opened the car's door and stepped out onto the gravel. The air was cool, but then, it was morning, in late September. The sun was warm, and she supposed that the day would be warmer once the sun had risen farther.

Holly leaned into the vehicle and picked up her small backpack. She'd packed a few granola bars, a sweater, a light jacket, and two bottles of water. Holly decided to wear the sweater, and promptly pulled it on. She was wearing walking shoes, which she felt would be adequate to the task, jeans, a flannel blouse, and now, the sweater. She slung the pack over her shoulder, stuck her mobile phone in her back pocket, and looked for the start of the trail she'd been told about. The parking lot boundary logs pointed the way. From where she stood, the trail looked well marked and she started on her way.

Holly and her boyfriend, Josh, had moved to the Denver area about six months ago. They had both worked at a bank in Florida, and when two positions came open in one of the company's Denver locations, Josh had convinced Holly they should move. Holly had acquiesced. She believed that the two of them would be engaged, although Josh kept saying he wanted to wait until they were a little more secure financially. That's the way Josh was. He was always thinking about having financial security before doing anything. She supposed she would be glad for that at some time in the future, but she wanted to know where her future lay.

Holly shook the thoughts from her head. There was no use thinking about that. Josh was at work and she was going to enjoy her day and her hike through the forest. Although the path was relatively flat and the incline slight, the added thousands of feet in elevation had thinned the air, and Holly found herself breathing heavily as she walked through the forest. She passed by a meadow on her right. She thought she saw a few deer at the far side and pulled out a small pair of binoculars to see them better. There were three deer. None had antlers, and she assumed that the two larger animals were does. A smaller one a fawn. As she pulled the binoculars from her eyes, she noted that clouds were forming, the sky now about half covered. Holly wasn't concerned. She knew from her short time she'd lived in the area that clouds often formed over the mountains in the afternoon. This was a little earlier, but she didn't think worrisome.

About a half hour after starting out, Holly came to a fork in the path. To the right, the path continued pretty much as it had been, flat, smooth, and wide. The path to the left appeared to be rougher and not as wide. Holly reasoned that a trail used by many, as this one was, would be the better one. Holly took the path to the right.

As she walked on, Holly didn't notice that the cloud layer had spread and thickened. The path wound through the forest and occasionally past meadows. An hour after taking the pathway to the right, the trail ended. She looked around and wandered in the area, but there was no continuation. Holly looked around, considering what to do. Feeling drained, she realized that her assumption about which trail was the right one had been wrong. She realized she had limited choices. She could turn around and back track to the parking lot. She would see the same scenery she'd seen on the way here. The scenery was beautiful, but she didn't want to fail in her goal to walk the trail loop. Since she had walked to the right, and the loop had turned to the left, Holly reasoned that if she turned to the left ninety degrees and headed through the forest, she would run into the loop trail in short order and she might not actually lose too much time. She might still be home by late afternoon, and she was determined to complete what she'd started out to do.

Holly turned to the left and started through the forest. There were frequent obstacles, and because of these, she had to take short and uneven strides to navigate the trees, rocks, and hillocks. As the case with most right-handed people, whenever Holly encountered an obstacle, she detoured slightly to the right. Ever so slowly, and without noticing it, Holly's route turned more and more to the right.

.

Two

In the KLMN television studio in Denver, the lights came on. The stand-in anchor took his seat and his assistant straightened his tie. He looked at the camera, and the director held up five fingers, which he used to count down to when the broadcast would go 'live.' The station's news bulletin music played in the background.

"Good afternoon. This is Bob Jenkins in the KLMN news room with a weather bulletin for all those in the Denver and western Colorado areas. A large and severe storm is building in the area and all residents should prepare for a heavy snow and a long storm. For more details, we switch now to meteorologist Sam Hale. Sam?"

"That's right Bob," the weatherman said as he pointed to a virtual map on his green screen. "We didn't really expect this to be as bad as it very well might be, but we've got cold – very cold – air racing down from Canada – coming farther and faster than we thought it would. At the same time, we've got this huge area of moisture coming up from the gulf. When they meet, and we expect that will be soon, there will be a large amount of snow here in the Denver area and even more in the mountains. If there is any good that will come out of this, it will be that the ski resorts will have a windfall of snow this year. Back to you, Bob."

"We'll keep you up to date, as well as we can. We suggest that if you don't have necessary supplies for the next few days, you should get them now. By the way, many businesses are closing early to make sure people are home safe before this storm makes travel impossible. This has been a KLMN weather news alert."

Three

Holly realized that the going was more difficult than she thought it would be. Her legs were tired, and her ankles sore. She'd come close to twisting one or both on multiple occasions. She couldn't understand why she hadn't connected with the loop trail. She did notice that it was getting colder, not warmer, as she'd assumed. There was no longer any sun shining through the occasional breaks in the evergreen canopy. And, she was starting to see snowflakes drift to the ground. At first, she thought, *Cool*, and caught a few on her tongue, but now she was becoming concerned that she might in fact be lost.

Holly trudged onward, chiding herself for not just backtracking. By now she was sure she would be back in her car, safe and warm, upset that she'd taken the wrong turn, but right now, she thought that was preferable. Her father had been a pilot and she remembered him saying on many occasions when he decided it was too risky to fly, "It's better to be on the ground wishing you were flying than in the air wishing you were on the ground." She thought that just might apply here, too.

The temperature had dropped significantly. And the wind had picked up – whistling through the trees. As soon as the snow had started falling, Holly had pulled the jacket out of her back pack and put it on. It provided some measure of relief, especially with the sweater she'd brought and she was thankful for it. Still, if it got much colder, Holly knew she might be in trouble – *unless I can find that stupid trail.* Holly's legs were a different matter. The thin denim material wasn't doing anything to keep the heat in or cold out.

The forest was starting to darken, and Holly realized that she had been out far longer than she'd planned. She wondered whether anyone would come looking for her. She remembered thinking it was a simple, short hike, and she hadn't even told anyone where she was headed. She might have told Josh, but he was absorbed in work. At least he knew she was going for a hike in the mountains. Mountains. Holly wondered how hard it would be to survive the night. *Oh, my god! I may be out here all night. I don't know what to . . .* Holly let the thought die. She wasn't sure she could face the prospect.

She heard something behind her and turned quickly to see what it might be. *Deer. There are deer out here.* She wondered how dangerous deer might be. She saw nothing. Then, she thought, *there are also cats – mountain lions. And wolves. And bears.* Suddenly, Holly was very afraid. She tried to keep herself from panicking, but she was on the edge.

There was another sound, and Holly jumped. All she could think of was a predator stalking her. She started running in the direction she had been going. She got about twenty feet, panting, when she tripped over something on the ground. She flew headfirst about ten feet, her torso landing on a hill. It knocked the breath out of her, and she lay still trying to catch her breath. After a few seconds, she realized she had landed on the bank of a stream. Her legs were in the water, up to mid-thigh. The water was so cold that her legs were already numb.

Holly scrambled out of the stream, now in almost full panic mode. Her legs were so cold that she wasn't feeling anything. She wondered whether she should take her jeans off. Would the cold be worse or better? She thought about being found in the forest with her pants off. She tried to think about what to do, but her mind wouldn't work. She realized that growing up in Florida hadn't prepared her for the dangers of even short hikes in the mountains. Or what to do in the cold. She knew she was in trouble and for the first time, she considered the very real possibility that she could die out here. She wondered whether her body would be found – or – or eaten by some animal.

Holly yelled for help. Over and over. It was useless, she knew, but she was beyond reason. Finally, she pulled herself over to a tree. She picked up a hefty stick, thinking it wouldn't protect her much if she was attacked by a wolf or bear, but she was determined not to go without a fight. Holly put her back against the tree and tried as best she could to pull her knees and legs under the jacket she was wearing. She took one look around, maybe the last of this earth she would see, and completely worn out, closed her eyes.

.

Four

Holly slowly became aware of herself. One of her first thoughts was to question whether she had died. She felt air going in and out of her as she breathed and decided that dead people probably didn't breathe. She opened her eyes slowly and saw something dark above her. It appeared to be a blanket – maybe. There was light, not a lot, but enough to see easily. Moving her eyes to look toward her feet, she saw she was in a sleeping bag. She rolled her head slightly to the right and saw a small pit in the ground surrounded by stones. In the center, a small fire burned. On the other side of the fire sat a man. Holly tried to focus. He was older. Trim. Wearing faded jeans and a light gray sweater. His hair was salt and pepper, with graying temples. He was reading a book, into which he placed a book mark, before closing it and setting it aside.

"Welcome back," he said in a soft voice. "You had me worried for a bit, but I thought you might be okay. Glad to see I was right – for a change."

"What – where?"

"This is my camp. We're way out in the boonies. When you feel more like talking, I'd like to know how you came to be this far out – dressed the way you were." He put a pot on a rack over the fire. "I set up camp a day and a half – maybe two days ago. I was getting ready to hunker down – big storm coming – and the wind died down for just a couple of seconds. I thought I heard someone calling for help. It might have just been a trick of the wind, but I decided to take a look. Found you huddled against a tree. About twenty yards away. If it had been much further, I might not have found you. Big stick in your hand. You were out. I tried to wake you, but you were really out. So, I carried you back here. I figured it would be better than freezing to death in the forest."

Holly turned on her side. She noticed that her clothes were gone and when she felt, she was wearing only some kind of a night shirt. "My clothes!"

"Yes. They were soaked. Your jeans were actually frozen. I had to get you warm, so I had to get you out of them. I had a long thermal underwear top. I put it on you after I got most of your wet things off – and slid off what was left after you were covered. A lady deserves her dignity. Your things are drying there."

Holly craned her neck and saw her clothes neatly arranged on a rack.

"It'll take a while for them to dry completely. But we're going to be here a while anyway. I have a feeling this storm is just cranking up."

"But," started Holly, "I have to call people to let them know I'm okay. I've got to get back to Denver. Tonight."

"Well, as far as calling, that's pretty much out of the question. Even if you hadn't taken your cell phone for a swim, there isn't any service up here. You can check with mine. As for getting out of here to pretty much anywhere, that isn't going to happen, either. There were six inches of snow on the ground when I found you. More like nine now, and it's still coming down. And, you can hear the wind. Trying to get anywhere in this would be committing suicide."

"Oh, NO!"

"You probably aren't happy about it, but you're, well we're pretty much stuck here until this is over and we can get you back to civilization. On the other hand, I'd say it was better than freezing to death in the forest. Water's hot. How about some broth?"

Holly was concerned about being stuck out here with a stranger, but then thought, *well, he did save my life. I suppose if he'd wanted to take advantage, he'd have done so already. And, when she'd awakened, he'd been reading a book, into which he'd placed a book mark.* Then, she wondered if all those things made her any safer.

As she was trying to figure it out, the man said, "I'm Pete. Pete Jackson. And you?"

"Oh. Holly. Holly Franklin." She tried to sit up and turn to face the fire.

"Here. Before you do that, I've got a set of trousers you can slip into. It'll make moving around, and especially getting out of that sleeping bag more, um, proper. You'll probably swim in them, no reference to your earlier activity intended, but you are a tiny thing."

"Thank you." Holly relaxed a bit, deciding that rapists and killers likely didn't allow their prey to dress before attacking them. "Um, before I have any of the broth, is there a – I mean I need to – uh – do you have a bathroom?"

Pete laughed. "Well, yes. You'll have to go out the back flap and about a step away you'll see a small tent. Inside there is a camp toilet. It won't be terribly warm, but it is better than trying to go to the bathroom sitting the captain's chair."

"Captain's chair?"

"Yeah. That's where you put our back against a tree with your knees at a ninety-degree angle. First, unless your legs are in really great shape, it doesn't take long before you're shaking and ready to collapse. Then too, it's hard to relax and do your thing when your legs are working that hard."

"So, outside?"

"Yes, I would have put it inside, but there would be obvious disadvantages to having a non-flush toilet inside the living space." Pete was smiling. "Here. Use this coat." Pete also handed her a flashlight.

Holly stepped out what Pete showed her was the back flap of the tent. Night had fallen, and it was dark. Two short steps away, through the snow, was a tent about the size of a phone booth. Opening the flap of the tent, she found a plastic toilet seat supported by three legs. A plastic bag hung underneath.

"I hope this thing supports me," she said to no one. Aside from the cold, the toilet seemed to work fine. She picked up a package with extra bags. There were instructions for use, and apparently, waste was sanitized as well as 'immobilized.' Wasting no extra time, Holly completed her task then without thinking, turned to flush. Then, she laughed at herself.

Five

Holly returned to the tent, glad for the warmth and light it provided.

Pete handed her an enameled cup filled with broth. She sipped it eagerly. She hadn't had anything to eat for – for hours, and the broth tasted and felt like heaven.

"So," began Pete, "forgive me for using an old worn out line, but what's a nice girl like you doing in a place like this?" Then, he laughed. Holly didn't quite understand and twisted her head to one side. "It's a line from about a hundred old movies," he said. "Guy meets a young lady, down on her luck, and she's working in some unsavory place and occupation. Just seemed appropriate for here."

"Oh." Holly then related how she and her boyfriend had come to the Denver area about six months ago but had been too busy to get up into the mountains much. She'd had the day off and decided on an easy hike that had turned out to be not so easy. "I didn't realize that I could get into trouble so fast," she finished.

"Well, I'm just very glad I was here and you basically stumbled upon my camp."

"Stumbled is right."

"Well, I get along fine up here. I know what the dangers are and prepare for them as best I can. I'm sure if I were to go the Florida and tried to camp out there, I'd make mistakes that would make you shake your head at my stupidity. But anytime you go into the mountains for any hike that could take you into an area you don't know, you should pack a few things.

Doesn't take too much. Coat, hat, gloves. Even in the summer, it gets cold at night up here. A tarp is good. You can use it to make a lean-to, or a pup tent of sorts. Something to start a fire. Emergency food and water. Basic first aid kit. Most all of that would have fit into your back pack. And, you'd be safer. I am glad to have you here, though."

"Really?"

"Yes. I usually come up here for the privacy. To get away from all the so-called civilized things in the world. Gives me time to think. Or read. And hike. This time, it felt like something was missing. At least until you came along."

"Thank you." Holly looked around at the inside of the tent. "Tell me about your tent."

"Well, it's called a teepee. The Native Americans had a good design. Spacious down here and no wasted space above. There's a vent in the top to allow the smoke from the fire to escape, so we can have light and fire here. Aluminum tent poles collapse and are easy to carry. A couple of layers of cover make it warm and cozy in here. And, I can knock it down and transport it with minimal effort. Ideal in many ways."

"And you do this . . ."

"Usually two or three times a year. I usually stay out a couple of weeks at a time."

"Do you always come here?"

"No. Actually, I move around. Different places. In a month or so, I'll probably head to the Red Feather Lakes area and camp in the Roosevelt National Forest. That time of year, there aren't many tourists."

"Doesn't your family object to you being gone so much?" asked Holly.

"No. No objections," said Pete as he looked down.

"I'm sorry. I think I . . . I didn't know. Can I help?"

"No. You couldn't know. And, there isn't really anything you could do."

Holly wanted to know. And, she wanted to help, whatever the problem was. But she decided to wait. The wind whistled through the trees outside, and the cover on the teepee shook.

"No need to worry. This thing is an old friend and has stood up to worse than this."

Holly looked at Pete. He looked to be trim and fit, although the baggy sweater didn't allow for much evaluation. When he moved in the tent, his movements were precise and smooth. His hair was salt and pepper, but neatly trimmed. His temples were graying, but his age was difficult to gauge. Her best guess was that he was about twice her age, but she couldn't be sure about that.

Wanting to change the subject, Holly asked, "How long do you think this will last?"

"Hard for us to tell. If we had a TV, or even a radio, although reception might not be very good right here, we'd get weather reports and have a better idea. The good news is, we've got enough sticks to keep the fire going for days and enough food that we won't starve."

"What's the bad news? There always seems to be bad news if there is good news," said Holly.

Pete looked at her, and she saw compassion in his eyes. "Bad news is the people who care about you won't know whether you're," he paused, searching for the right way to say it, "okay or not for a few days. They'll likely be very worried. Good news there is that you are actually okay. And, you'll be back with them in a few days. Still, for them, it will be a rough few days."

Any concerns she might have had about Pete dissolved. Not only had he saved her and taken care of her, but he seemed to be genuinely concerned for her feelings and those of the people who cared about her. She leaned back and watched the flames flicker. She was suddenly very thankful and interested in the simple things that make up life.

Six

Pete made dinner. He wrapped small Yukon gold potatoes, cut green beans, and ground beef into aluminum foil and set them in the fire. "I apologize. If I knew I was going to have company, I would have brought something a little fancier," he said.

"Please. Don't apologize. I'm lucky to be alive, warm, and well. Anything to eat will be great. To tell the truth, I'm starved and I'm looking forward to this meal."

After a half hour or so, Pete checked the meals. Everything seemed to be done, so he pulled out both, opened them and put the contents of each into an enamel bowl as kind of a stew. Holly's stomach was doing flip-flops at the thought of a meal. Then too, it smelled delicious.

"Now don't expect too much. I'm not a great cook," said Pete.

Holly took her first bite. "Oh my, I can't imagine anything better than this." And she meant it. The day, the cold, then being saved made a simple meal incredible.

"Well, I guess if I want more compliments on my cooking, I'll have to arrange to find a half-starved, half-frozen woman to thaw out." Pete laughed, then Holly joined in.

After dinner, Pete made some herbal tea. Holly's new-found appreciation for the simple things found her very happy and satisfied. Soon, Pete started pulling a few more sticks out of his stash. He piled them relatively close to, but not in, the fire. "So I can just roll over and put one or two in as need be while we're asleep tonight. Don't want the fire to go out. We want to keep it warm in here. We could do without the fire if need be, but it will be more comfortable with it going."

Holly had finished her tea and was wondering what the sleeping arrangements would be.

"If you need to use the convenience before you go to bed, this would be a good time," he said.

Holly steeled herself, threw on a jacket, and headed for the latrine. When she returned, Pete had the sleeping bag ready for her. "Just climb in and pull off those trousers. Keep the long johns on. They'll help keep you warm, but contrary to popular belief, keeping all your clothes on while sleeping out in the wilds," he smiled, "will make you feel colder."

"Are you going to," she started to ask.

"I'll bunk down on the other side of the fire. I've got a couple of blankets that should keep me warm."

Holly noticed that he was fully dressed, including boots. "You don't look like you're taking your own advice about wearing everything while you sleep."

"Well, sometimes," he started.

"Wait a minute. I understand now. You're giving me your sleeping bag. You're going to be out in the cold. Right?"

"I wouldn't say that . . ."

"But it's true. You're going to be cold because I'm going to be nice and warm."

"Well," he started reluctantly, "you need to be warm. You're not used to this. It's cold, and if I'm right, it is getting colder. I can't let you get cold. You've already had a major shock to your system. If anything happened . . ."

"This is NOT acceptable," Holly said. "We've got to find some way for you to sleep inside this bag, too." Holly stared at Pete for a minute then said, "Oh my god! You think I might be afraid, I might be worried about you being that close to me?"

"You are a young lady who is – is practically engaged to be married to another man. It just wouldn't be proper . . ."

"I'll tell you what isn't proper. It isn't proper for you to sit out in the cold after all you've done for me. You shouldn't – no, make that I won't allow it."

"So, just what do you suggest?"

"I suggest that if you want to use the convenience, now would be a good time. Then, I suggest, you get yourself over here and into what was supposed to be and what will be your nice warm bed."

When Pete returned from the convenience, he removed his boots and started to slip into the bag in his clothes.

"An expert in camping told me that in order to keep warm, you shouldn't sleep with all your clothes on," Holly said, then smiled.

"You don't give a fellow a break, do you? In case you haven't noticed, I'm more than a little nervous here."

"Why?"

"For a whole lot of reasons I'd rather not talk about right now. Is that okay?" Pete slowly removed his jacket, sweater, and trousers, leaving his long johns and socks on.

"You don't have to be nervous," said Holly, thinking that his being nervous was cute. "I'll be right here by your side all night to make sure everything is okay."

"That's kind of what is making me nervous."

"Oh, pshaw. I won't hurt you," then, she added with a smile, "and I hardly ever bite."

Pete groaned. Holly laughed. Then, Pete slid into the sleeping bag and zipped it closed to neck level.

Seven

The sleeping bag was more spacious than Holly thought. There was room for both of them and a little space between them, as well. The day had taken its toll. It wasn't long before Holly was sound asleep.

At some point, Holly had a dream. Actually, more of a bad dream, if not a nightmare. She was lost in a fog. Everything was white. She couldn't see anything in any direction, but even more worrisome, she couldn't move. In her dream, she tried to yell, but no sound came out of her mouth. She had a feeling that something was wrong. Slowly, in front of her, some of the fog cleared. She could see a form. As the fog cleared more, she saw the form was her boyfriend, Josh. He was sitting at a desk with his back turned to her. He was wearing a suit and counting piles of money on the desk. Holly tried to yell, but no sound came out of her mouth. She was desperate to get his attention. He wouldn't turn. Then, she saw Pete. He was standing in front of Josh. He was yelling although there was no sound either. Pete was yelling and pointing toward Holly, but Josh just looked back down to the desk and kept counting. Holly was starting to panic, some sense of danger looming. Then, Pete was next to her and engulfed her. First with his arms and then completely. The sense of danger disappeared.

Holly woke in a sweat. The dream had rattled her. *Just what did it all mean?* She felt upset and alone. Cautiously, she moved closer to Pete, who was sleeping soundly. Their bodies touched. She could feel the warmth of him. Knowing he was there and that he would protect her, Holly relaxed. She fell asleep in seconds and slept without dreams or waking for the rest of the night.

Holly and Pete woke about the same time the next morning. It took Holly a minute or so to reorient herself to where she was and her situation. About the same time, she also realized she had draped her arm over Pete. He was on his back, and her arm lay across his chest. Slowly, carefully, she retrieved her arm, noting as she did that even if he was older than her by a good measure, he still appeared to be in good shape. He was trim, and his muscles felt solid. Her chest was against his arm, and his upper arms were good-sized and firm. She started to roll away – slowly.

When Pete spoke, Holly jumped. "So, would this be a good time to talk about some of those reasons I was nervous?"

"What? Look. See. Oh, pook. I got nothing," and with that, she laughed. Then, she said, "Look. We spent the night in close proximity . . ."

"I see you chose not to say we slept together."

"Well, sleeping with someone isn't any big deal, except that when most people say 'sleeping together,' they don't really mean they were sleeping. They were actually wide awake. So, yes, I chose not to use those words. But nothing happened, we were both fully clothed, at least covered, and we both stayed warm. By the way, I woke up sometime during the night and you seemed to be sleeping just fine."

"You win, counsellor. The prosecution concedes." Pete smiled. "I actually woke slightly three times during the night – it's kind of automatic out here, you know to put a stick or two on the fire to keep it going. I didn't have the heart to wake you. You seemed peaceful."

"So, I was, um . . ."

"Draped. Let's call it draped."

"So, I was next to you, close to you, and you didn't move me away?"

"Yes. Let's say you were draped on me and I didn't have the heart to move you. I didn't want to wake you."

"Okay, so I was close to you and we had a nice comfortable and proper night's sleep."

"I'm not sure your boyfriend would consider it quite proper."

Holly thought about her dream. "You know, I'm not sure he would care."

"Then forgive me for saying this, but your boyfriend would be a fool."

They got out of the sleeping bag and dressed. Pete asked if he could use the convenience first. When it was Holly's turn, she saw that Pete had thrown a tarp over a rope connecting the convenience to the teepee. So, in going to the convenience, she didn't have to trudge through the snow. He said he'd put two candles in the smaller tent, and she was to blow them out after she finished. The result was that the little toilet room, while not warm, was at least ten to fifteen degrees warmer than it would have been.

When Holly returned to the teepee, Pete was fixing breakfast – eggs and bacon – over the fire. After those were done, he used a grill of sorts to toast some bread.

"You should open a restaurant," Holly said. "I've never eaten so well."

"A few days back in civilization, and you will wonder just what it was that was so special here."

Holly started to answer, but when she looked at him all she could think was, *I know what is so special here. It's a man who saved my life and is so considerate that he's trying to heat up the toilet. Not to mention, he was going to stay on the other side of the tent, cold, while I slept warm and safe.*

"No. I'll remember. I'll remember everything." She was looking at him.

He averted his eyes and said, "So, tell me about this boyfriend."

"Josh?"

"Do you have another one, as well?"

"No. Sorry. Well, I grew up in Florida – you know, the place where I learned all my mountaineering skills. Josh and I met in college. We were both business majors. When we graduated, we stayed together. Got jobs at different branches of the same bank. We've talked about getting engaged, but Josh says that he wants to be financially stable first. So, he can get all the things that will make me happy."

"Seems to me, the thing that will make a woman happy is spending time with the man she loves. When time is gone, you can't get it back. When things are gone, you can always get more things. If you've spent your time trying to get things, and the one you love is lost, then . . . then all those 'things' only serve as a reminder that you were a fool not to spend your time with the one thing – the person - who really mattered. Anything that gets in the way of the relationship – time together – can wait until later." He studied the blanket on the ground for a minute. "And, then?"

"And then, two positions opened at a branch in the Denver area. Josh thought that would be ideal."

"What did *you* think?"

"What?"

"What did you think? I mean it sounds like you had roots in Florida. Did you talk about what the move would mean to you?"

"I guess I got caught up in the whole thing. I mean, I assumed we would be engaged, then married. So far, that hasn't quite worked out."

"Seems to me, and forgive me for butting in where I don't have any business, you need to find a way to make it work out. Or find something that will work out."

Now, both were studying the blanket on the ground.

Finally, Pete said, "Okay. Time for me to get cleaned up."

"Cleaned up?"

"Yup. Shave, shower, and shampoo."

"Excuse me? I didn't see the shower when I entered this fine establishment. Please tell me it's not outside. I think I'd rather stay dirty."

Pete laughed. "No, it's not that bad. Sponge bath, then shampoo. Usually, I just strip down – outside if the weather is warm – in here if it's like this. Heat some water over the fire, and voila! You're clean. Since I have company I wasn't expecting, I think we can rig a blanket, or the sleeping bag, to give some privacy. I'll explain how to do it, and either go first, or let you."

"Do you have enough water?"

Pete laughed again. "Water? There's at least two feet of it for acres just outside the tent flap."

So, Pete heated water over the fire, showing Holly how to do it before she disappeared behind the makeshift curtain. She stripped out of her clothes and completed the sponge bath in a relatively few minutes. She washed her hair, dressed in clean briefs and t-shirt, both of which were provided by Pete. Then, it was his turn, with Holly heating the water and placing it behind the curtain. In addition to the sponge bath, Pete also shaved.

Eight

After rearranging the inside of the tent, Pete said, "Time to get dinner."

"You going to the store?"

"In a manner of speaking. Want to come along?"

"This I want to see. If there's a supermarket close by, I'm going to want to know just what we've been doing."

Pete dressed in his outdoor gear. He gave Holly an extra coat and a pair of mukluks he kept on hand. They walked out the front flap. The day was gray and quiet. Snow was still falling, but Holly could see about ten yards. Pete started out in the snow, and Holly followed, stepping in the trough he was making as he walked through the snow. About twenty yards from the tent, he stopped. Holly looked around.

"Now what?" she asked.

"We're at the store."

Holly saw nothing. Then, Pete looked straight up. Twenty feet above the ground, a large sack was suspended from a tree limb. A rope looped over a branch and down around the tree. It was tied off about five feet above the ground.

"Your refrigerator?"

"Yes, all that, and more. You see, there are predators in this area. You know, mountain lions. Bears. Bears are about the worst. Anyway, if you keep your food right next to you, and a bear decides he – or she – wants something to eat, well, that is trouble. This way, the food isn't near us, and in a place difficult for the bear to get, as well."

Pete undid the rope and lowered the sack. He pulled out a couple of packages and hoisted the sack back into the air. They retraced their steps to the tent. Inside, they stripped off the outdoors wear.

"So, how did you learn that little trick?"

"Last woman I rescued? Left a sandwich in her backpack. The results were . . ." he turned away, feigning grief.

"REALLY!? That really happened?"

Pete turned around laughing. "I am going to have to be so careful with you. I can't believe you thought that was true."

Holly punched him softly in the stomach. Her fist met hard muscles. Trim, hard muscles. "I'll get you. I swear, I'll get you for this one." But she was laughing, too.

Dinner was white chili. It was seasoned mildly. "Hope you don't mind mild seasoning. I never did like things so spicy you couldn't taste the food itself."

"No. This is perfect," answered Holly. "Besides, what kind of a guest would I be if I complained about the free food. Especially after being saved by you."

"Well, I'm glad if it suits you. And, thank you if you're lying so I won't have my feelings hurt."

They ate in silence for a bit. Then, Holly said, "This has got to be the longest time I've ever been without – you know, television, radio, all that."

"And, how's it going?"

"I would like to know how long this storm is going to last, but it's funny. I'm kind of enjoying being away from all that. Is that strange? Is that why you come out here?"

"Oh, there are a few reasons I come out here."

"So, if you come out here for the solitude, I guess I messed that up for you." Holly giggled and said, "If you'd left me out there, you wouldn't have had your privacy violated. And have had to put up with me."

Pete stopped eating and looked at her. Holly thought the look was sad. Very sad. "First, I've enjoyed your company – very much." He paused.

"If there's a first, there's got to be at least a second."

"Okay. Second, I couldn't have left you there even if it would have meant my life." He put his head down and took a bite of his dinner.

After a long pause, Holly looked at him and said, "I want to know about you. It's not like you owe it to me. After all, you saved me. Now you're feeding me. But you know about me. I want to know about you."

"Well, young lady, I do seem to know a little about you. I wonder how little I can tell you about me."

"I don't want to know a little about you. I want to know all about you."

He looked at Holly. She wasn't smiling. She was looking at him like she was engrossed, interested. Maybe a little sad.

"Okay. Let's not start with my birthdate." That brought a small smile to Holly's face. "You probably want to know how I got here."

"Please don't say you drove in your truck, van, whatever. You know, parked twenty feet from here on the highway."

Pete smiled a slight smile. "No." He paused for a full minute. Maybe two. To Holly, it seemed like a long time. "I guess in a way, I was like your boyfriend. I hate to admit it. I was married. Helen was her name. I loved her and she loved me. I had – a business. I wanted to build the business so she could have all the important things in life. Sound familiar? Once we got some money and financial security, we were going to cut back. Travel. Relax. Do nothing but enjoy each other's company. But that was for later. At the time, I was working fourteen to sixteen-hour days. Helen would come to see me at work when she could. Looking back, it wasn't as much as I would have liked. But she believed in me and supported me completely. I tried not to disappoint her, but I'm sure that on occasion, I did."

Pete took a sip of tea and thought for a minute or two. "Then, one day, she was gone."

"She left?" asked Holly.

"In a manner of speaking. She passed."

Holly gasped. "Oh my . . ."

"I didn't even have a chance to say goodbye. It was devastating. I tried to keep busy and bury myself in my work, but it didn't work. Everything I'd worked for, hoped for, was gone."

"Did you ever try to . . ." Holly started to ask.

"Find someone else? It's not like replacing a dead goldfish. At first, it's like a sledgehammer to your chest. People tell you it will get better with time. Mostly, they are people who don't know. You see, while you – kind of – deal with that pain, others take their place. Little things peck at you. You don't get coffee brought to you while you're shaving for work. You don't have to put up with a dinner you don't really care for because you never had the heart to tell her it wasn't your favorite. There isn't someone there to steal your covers in the middle of the night, then apologize in the morning. A thousand little things that you don't even realize – then you miss terribly."

Holly was staring.

"The worst. The absolute worst is when something really exciting happens and the first thing you do is turn to tell her about it – she's the one you want to know – and it takes a few seconds to realize that she is no longer there." If Pete had a sad look on his face, Holly was crying. Big tears were rolling down her face, landing on her jeans.

"Of course, there were women, it seemed like plenty of women, who were interested in taking her place. Most were more interested in my bank balance than how much sugar to put into my tea. So, I decided to sell the, er, business and do something else. I had no interest or motivation to continue, so it was for the best. You want to hear the funny part?"

"I can't imagine anything being funny in this," said Holly.

"When I checked my retirement portfolio, after selling the business, I had enough money that we could have done all the things we wanted. Later. Later is the enemy of doing what you should now. Later is the enemy of a satisfying life. Do those important things now. Save the junk for later. Save the unimportant for later. You never know when the road to 'later' will run out."

Holly came around the fire, stayed on her knees, and wrapped her arms around Pete. "Oh, I'm so sorry. I didn't know. I – I . . ."

"It's okay, Holly. I've been dealing with it for a long time. And yes, it is why I come out here. Not just for the solitude, although it is nice to get away from all the crap in the cities. I come out here to be alone with myself. To think and reflect. To re-create who I am. It isn't a sentence. It's actually a pleasure. Alone. In nature."

"God! And I even managed to screw that up! I'm sorry. If I hadn't been so stupid."

"If you hadn't been, as you put it 'so stupid,' I would have missed out on meeting a wonderful young woman. You've actually brought a great deal of joy into this trip and my life. So, thank you for that."

"You're not just saying that so I won't feel bad?"

"No. I generally don't do those sorts of things. And I wouldn't do that to you, in any case."

Darkness had fallen, and Pete said it was probably best to hit the sack. They took turns heading to the convenience and Pete pulled out more sticks to feed the fire during the night. Holly slid into the sleeping bag first, then Pete slid in and zippered it closed. He stayed close to the zipper, trying to give Holly the room she needed and keep some separation between them. He felt Holly snuggle up behind him and drape one arm over his side and onto his stomach. Pete tensed up.

"Um," he started, "you, uh . . ."

"Shush," she responded. "It's bed time and not time to talk. You might as well relax. I'm not going to move away. And I'm not going to attack you. It's warmer this way, and I feel more comfortable. Think of this as one of those things you'll miss about me when I'm gone." Holly regretted saying it as soon as she did, fearing it would bring back sad memories.

She felt Pete relax and heard him quietly say, "Oh, Lord."

Nine

The next morning, Holly woke slowly. When consciousness had fully returned, she didn't want to move. Sometime in the night, she had rolled over and was now facing the tent wall. The reason she didn't want to move was that Pete had also rolled over. She was curled up, and he was curled around her. His arm was draped over her. She was cocooned, and she loved the feeling. A tingling ran through her from head to toe. It brought back a memory of sitting on the couch as a little girl. It was a snowy morning, and she was sipping hot chocolate, with marshmallows. It was that, plus the tingling she didn't experience as a little girl. She drifted off again and had the most marvelous dream.

Sometime later, she felt Pete leave her side and get out to the convenience. When she rolled over, he was heating water over the fire. Holly looked at him and smiled.

"Morning," he said. "Look. I hope I didn't – I mean I didn't want to . . ."

Holly giggled and Pete stopped in mid-sentence and stared at her. "Oh my god!" she said. "You're embarrassed! I can't believe . . . I mean, you're a perfect gentleman. Besides, I really liked having you – what was the word – draped. Yes, that was it, draped over me. Warm and safe."

Pete was turning bright red, so Holly crawled out of the sleeping bag, went to him, gave him a big hug and kiss on the cheek. "Thank you, sir, for a warm and cozy night." He seemed to relax. "Draped in your arms." And she giggled again. This time, Pete just rolled his eyes.

Holly used the convenience. When she returned, Pete handed her a cup. In it, she was surprised to find hot chocolate with marshmallows. *This is almost like a dream come true*, she thought. "If only we had a couch and blanket," she whispered.

"What?" asked Pete.

"Nothing. Just an old memory. A really good one. Hot chocolate under a blanket on the couch. It was also a snowy morning." *But I didn't get to spend the night before that morning wrapped by a dreamy guy,* she thought, *or have that tingly feeling, either. This might actually be better.*

Ten

In the KLMN television studio in Denver, the lights came on. The stand-in anchor took his seat. His assistant straightened his tie and checked his makeup. He looked at the camera, and the director held up five fingers, which he used to count down to when the broadcast would go 'live.' The station's news bulletin music played in the background.

"Good afternoon. This is Bob Jenkins in the KLMN news room with a news bulletin for all those in the Denver and western Colorado areas. The large and severe storm we've experienced in the area has dumped at least twelve inches of snow in the Denver area, significantly more in the foot hills and at elevation. For more details, we switch now to meteorologist Sam Hale. Sam?"

"That's right Bob," the weatherman said as he pointed to a virtual map on his green screen. "As we told you on Tuesday, this storm has materialized and dropped a large amount of heavy, wet snow on the entire area. We expect conditions will improve tomorrow and we should have full sun, and some melting of this by the weekend. For the latest, get the KLMN weather app on your mobile device. Back to you, Bob."

The camera changed to catch the news anchor, "As you can imagine, thousands are without power in the area due to downed trees and in some cases, due to heavy snow on the power lines. If you are listening to this broadcast, you have power, so please go to our website and see the things you should do to keep yourself safe."

"In another news item, a hiker has not been heard from in three days. Holly Franklin hiked into the Roosevelt National Forest on Tuesday and hasn't been heard from since. Holly is twenty-nine years old. She has red hair and green eyes. Five feet four inches tall and weighs one hundred and thirty pounds. Crews won't be able to start searching until the storm passes, but we ask if anyone has seen Holly, please call this station or the local police or fire station."

"We'll keep you up to date, as well as we can. We suggest that if you don't have the necessary supplies for the next few days, you should get them now if you can. Many businesses are closed and as with any storm, supplies are running low in the stores. This has been a KLMN news alert."

Eleven

Pete fixed eggs and bacon again. The toast came a bit later. "Hard to get it all done at one time," he said as an apology.

"This is unbelievable. I can't remember breakfast tasting this good," said Holly.

"Well, to tell the truth," responded Pete, "I've found that camping out makes pretty much anything taste pretty good. And, of course," he said with a smile, "almost freezing to death after getting lost will give you a new appreciation for pretty much anything in life."

"Still," said Holly with a mouthful, "this is great."

"Why thank you, Ma'am. I'll be sure to pass the compliment along to the management."

After a pause, Holly asked, "So now that you're independently wealthy . . ."

"What do I do with my time?"

"Exactly."

"Well, I hate to deflate your party balloon, but I'm not independently wealthy. I'm okay, but I still watch my money. I don't drive a big fancy car. My home is modest."

"How many bedrooms?"

"Four."

"Why so many?"

"I don't know. I guess it just worked out that way. One I use for an office. One is actually my bedroom."

"And the other two?"

"Guest rooms, although I don't seem to have any guests. I think I bought the house in the days when I was still thinking about what Helen and I would do, even if she wasn't around anymore."

"Land?"

"Four acres."

"Sounds pretty nice to me."

"Well, it would be much more expensive if I had a Rodeo Drive address, but it isn't."

"Okay, but back to my question. What do you do?"

"I write. I do a bit of volunteer work."

"What do you write?"

"A couple of things. I do some technical writing. And, I write fiction."

"What kind of fiction?"

"Novels."

"Genre?"

"You're kind of nosey for a house guest, you know."

"Teepee guest, and why don't you want to tell me about the genre?"

"Fine. I write romance novels."

"Cool. I love romance fiction. Do you use your name, or a nom de plume?"

"P. D. Jackson. I had a model pose for the picture with me. She's looking at the camera. I'm looking at her. Most people think she's the author. That's fine with me."

"I've read your stuff. It's good. I like it."

"Thank you."

"And volunteer work?"

"Yes."

Holly rolled her eyes. "You know, getting information out of you is like pulling teeth."

"I've got friends who are dentists, and they say that pulling teeth is kind of fun."

"You're exasperating. But don't worry. I'm like the splinter you get that you can't quite get out. Irritating, never leaving you in peace. Until you answer my questions, that is. That's when you can have your peace."

Pete just looked at her with wide eyes.

"And, somewhat of a closet pervert, I see. That's not what I meant." Holly was smiling broadly.

"I can only respond to what you say. Your choice of words and phraseology left some doubt as to the interpretation."

"Fine. We'll call that one a draw."

"I didn't know we were keeping track," he said.

"Women always keep track," responded Holly, "unless we aren't winning. Then, we'll tell you we aren't keeping track. But, we are. So?"

"I volunteer at a clinic – and before you ask, they provide free medical care to people who can't afford it."

"I'm glad to see that you have learned I get the information I want. Now, what do you do at this clinic?"

Pete took a deep breath and let it out. "I'm a physician."

"Like doctor!?" Now, Holly had wide eyes.

"Yes."

Holly was silent for a long time. Finally, she said, "So it was a medical practice that you were building – for the future."

"Yes. A future that never came."

Holly wanted to know more, but she sensed that she had probed enough. Pete was deep in thought and disturbing him would only make him sadder.

After a bit, he said, "Time to go to the store again. How about fish for dinner?"

"Sounds great. Mind if I tag long?

"No. I'll be happy to have you."

Soon, they were trudging through the snow.

Twelve

Pete led Holly back to the cache of food. Just before they arrived, Pete stopped short and froze.

"What?" asked Holly.

"Shush. Just listen."

After a minute, Holly whispered, "What are we listening for?"

Pete looked around carefully, then lowered the food. "We'll grab this fast and head back to the tent. I've got some things to do."

"What's the problem?"

Pete pointed to the other side of the tree. "See those holes in the snow? Those are bear tracks."

"Bear tracks? Are we going to get to see a bear?" Holly seemed excited at the prospect.

"Uh, this isn't the zoo. They aren't behind bars or walls. Just to let you know, sometimes they consider us part of the food chain."

Holly's joy and excitement ended immediately. "So, what do we do?"

"First, we're going to set up an early warning line – to let us know if there are any intruders. Then, we're going to take some precautions."

Pete grabbed what food he wanted and they headed back toward the tent. Pete was looking all around as they went.

As soon as they were back at camp, Pete got some line. He went out and Holly watched as he circled the tent – at a distance – running the line around a tree perimeter. When he finished that, he attached little jingle bells in various places on the line. "In case we have any visitors, this should give us a little warning."

"If a bear shows up, what are we going to do – run?"

"Before you run from something, you should figure out if you can out run it. In this case, we can't. No, we're not running. If we ran, we'd be running out into the forest, in the dark, with no protection against the cold. Or anything that might be waiting for us."

"All of a sudden, this doesn't seem like fun anymore."

"We'll be fine. I'll take care of you." Pete was smiling.

"What if anything happens to you," Holly asked.

"In that case, pray that by the time they are done eating me they'll be full."

"Oh, God!"

They went back into the tent. Pete went into the back corner and returned with a box. When he opened it, Holly saw a large gun – like the ones in westerns, only bigger.

"What's that?"

"Our last resort. It's called a Ruger – Super Blackhawk. It shoots a big bullet. With enough power to take down a bear."

"You're going to shoot him?"

"Only if I really have to. I'll try to persuade him – or her – to leave quietly. As a second last resort, I'll fire one shot into the air. I the bear persists, I may have no choice. I don't plan on becoming bear scat. And, if he gets me, you'll be next, and I can't let that happen."

Pete loaded the gun, put it into a holster, and placed the holster at the side of the tent, within reach. The muzzle was pointed toward the side of the tent.

Dinner was fish along with bread. They made sandwiches. Pete opened a can of peas. "Always have to have your veggies, you know." Holly was surprised he could be so relaxed.

"How can you be so relaxed?" she asked. "My nerves are frazzled."

"We're pretty well prepared. The bear may not return. If it does, I may be able to scare it off. We've done everything we can."

"And, the gun – if you have to shoot him?"

"That gun will do the job. It's made to take down big animals. I'll only use it if I have to. And, remember the first shot – most likely – will be an attempt to scare the bear away. Big gun, big noise. They'll hear it in the next state."

Thirteen

They were sitting and relaxing after they finished their dinner. Night had fallen. After dinner, Pete had cleaned the dishware, neatened the inside of the teepee and made tea. He also strapped on the holster for the pistol but left the pistol on the ground. They were about half-way through their tea when they heard the sound of the jingle bells ringing. Holly jumped. Pete calmly put down his tea.

"I'll check. You stay here," he said. Pete picked up a flashlight, holstered the pistol, and grabbed something else. He turned and smiled at Holly, then stepped through the tent flap. All Holly heard was the sound of the wind through the trees.

The tent flap opened slowly. Holly's eyes were riveted on it. Pete stepped through.

"Oh, thank god!" she said.

"Just a deer. Passing through." Then, he sat back down and picked up his tea.

"How can you do this?" Holly asked.

"Do what?"

"Seem so relaxed. Every sound makes me want to jump out of my skin."

"Training, I guess."

"How do you train for something like this?"

"Sometimes as a physician, you have to wait for things to happen before you can start to work. You learn to take the down times as they come and relax. Then, too, years ago." The thought trailed off.

"Years ago, what?"

Pete jumped slightly, as if startled out of a deep thought.

"Doesn't matter now."

"Remember the splinter in the finger I told you about?" asked Holly.

"Fine. Years ago, before I went to school and became a doctor, I was a Marine."

Holly sat riveted. "I was what is called a designated marksman. It's like being a sniper without all the stalking training. Just somebody who is a very good marksman. If the company or squad needed a precision shot at a long distance, they called on the DM."

"Did you . . ."

"Yes. That's why I decided to become a doctor when I got out. To save lives rather than take them. And that's one of the reasons I'll try to scare the bear rather than shoot it."

"If the bear comes back, can I see it?"

"If the bear comes back and everything goes according to plan, I'll take you to the zoo where you can see one safely."

"Well, don't you think . . ." She was interrupted by the sound of the jingle bells going off again. Holly's eyes flashed to the tent flap.

"Stay here and be quiet." Pete disappeared through the tent flap.

For a minute there was no sound. Holly was hoping it was another deer. Then, Pete was yelling, telling whatever it was to go away. Then, there was a bang, not a loud bang, but loud enough. Holly wondered if that was the gun going off.

In a minute, Pete emerged from the outside.

"Are you okay? Was it the bear?"

"Yeah. A young one. As soon as I set off the flash-bang, he took off."

"Flash-bang?"

"Yeah. It's harmless enough, a smaller version of what the police use. It makes a bright flash and a bang. The big ones stun bad guys and give the police a few seconds to take them down. The little ones I have just scare the bejeesus out of animals and make them run away. I don't think he'll be back, but I'm going to guard the outside in case he gets curious."

"It's getting colder. I don't want you to stay out too long. Understand?"

"Yes, dear. Just keep the fire going. I'll probably want another cup of tea when I come in." And he was back outside.

Holly worried about the cold, but she figured he knew what he was doing. She put a few more sticks on the fire, then, the stress of the day overwhelmed her and she drifted off to sleep. She dreamt she was back at work in the bank. Everyone was a stranger. She didn't know anyone. Finally, Josh came out of an office. When she ran to him for comfort, he didn't seem to know her, or care about her. He was talking with men in suits.

Holly woke with a start. The fire that had been so warm and bright was now just a few flickering sticks. She added more, and the flames started to grow. But, she realized that she must have fallen asleep for some time, and Pete was nowhere to be found. Suddenly, she was in a panic.

Holly threw on her coat and stepped into the cold night air. The coldness shocked her. And she was blind in the darkness. She called out Pete's name, but there was no response. She called again. Nothing. She was really starting to panic when her eyes started to adjust. It was dark, but the whiteness of the snow started to provide a minimum amount of light. She looked around wildly for any sign of Pete. Finally, about twenty feet away, she saw what she thought might be him sitting by a tree.

"You could at least answer me," she started. "I was scared half to death – not knowing if you were here, or hurt, or something. Pete?" Then, she noticed he was not responding. She reached for his hand. There was no response. "Oh God! Oh, please God." She pulled her hand out of her glove and put the back of it against his face. He was ice cold. "Oh, please God. Oh, please God."

Holly grabbed the hood of his coat and pulled. Pete toppled over. Holly dropped onto her knees in the snow and rolled Pete onto his back. Then, she stood and started pulling him toward the tent using the hood of his coat. It was a struggle, and it seemed to take an hour, but it was most likely only a few minutes. Once inside the tent, the fire was still increasing, so Holly figured it had been less than five minutes.

Pete felt cold to the touch. He didn't respond, and she knew she shouldn't try to get him something hot to drink.

Then, she remembered a television special she'd seen as a little girl. When Eskimos would revive someone who had suffered from hypothermia, they would put them under blankets and climb under the blankets with them. Of course, everyone under the blankets was naked. It seemed like a small price to pay. Holly undressed Pete, and even under the circumstances saw that he was indeed in great shape. She rolled him into the sleeping bag, then removed her clothing, as well. Climbing in next to him, she felt the coldness in is body. She thought to herself, *you know, I wouldn't do this for just anybody.* Then, she started praying that he would recover.

.

Fourteen

Pete's body had warmed and the shivering bouts that came with the body's attempt to warm itself had slowed and were coming only infrequently. Holly rested her head on his chest and could hear the slow rhythmic beating of his heart. She saw that the small fire had diminished and reached out of the sleeping bag to add a few sticks. She turned back and rested her arm across Pete's chest. She thought about the last few days. Here was a man she hadn't known — hadn't known existed — who saved her life, then risked his to make sure she was safe. She also noted how perfectly her body fit against his. She thought about Josh. Would he have done either of those things in order to save her? She wasn't sure.

Pete slowly opened his eyes. He looked at Holly, who was looking up at him. It registered that they were both wrapped in the sleeping bag, naked together.

"I have a question," he started.

"You were outside. Guarding me, keeping me from getting killed and eaten by a bear. But you stayed out too long. If I hadn't gone out and looked . . ."

"I get it — Pete-cicle."

"I pulled you in as best I could. And got you out of those clothes."

"Okay, I'm with you so far."

"I remember reading that when someone almost freezes to death — by the way, that was you. Anyway, I remember seeing that the Eskimos would take all their clothes off and climb under covers, using their naked body heat to revive the, in this case, almost dead guy."

"Okay, so I'm kind of caught up. I've got to tell you, though, when I started coming around and found out there was a young, beautiful woman naked beside me, I thought I was either dreaming a great dream or dead and in heaven. Truth be known, if that was heaven, I wouldn't have minded being dead at all."

"So," she said, "that pretty much makes us even. When I woke up here the other day, I thought I'd died and gone to heaven. By the way, thank you for the beautiful."

"The truth is the truth, and heaven it is," he said. "Might still be heaven if that boyfriend of yours comes through the tent flap and doughnut holes us both with a twelve gauge."

"Doughnut holes. That's cute. Josh? No. Josh isn't the kind to, as you say, doughnut hole anyone. He might be hurt, sure, but he'd probably calculate what each response might mean for his lifestyle and financial future."

"That can't be true."

"You know, until I said it, I didn't really realize that it was true. But I'm pretty sure it is."

"That's pretty sad. Really sad." After a minute Pete said, "So, did you want to get out of this bag and into something else?"

"Actually," said Holly, "if it's all the same to you, I'm really comfortable here. Could we just stay like this for a bit?" Then, she smiled and said, "At least until Josh arrives, that is. Then, we should definitely get up."

"Pete laughed and said, "Sure. But I'm not really dressed for company."

Both were laughing. The situation was funny. The comments were funny. All of a sudden, they weren't. Holly looked up at Pete. She thought, *here's a man who saved my life and risked his. He listens when I talk and is truly interested in me and what I want.* Holly stretched just a bit and kissed Pete softly on his lips. She kissed him softly again, and this time he returned her soft kiss. Holly moved her hand to his stomach and played her fingers back and forth. There was another of those shivers, but Holly didn't think it had to do with the cold. She moved her hand further down his body and found that he was already starting to respond.

"I'm not sure you should," he started to say.

"Shush! I don't want to talk right now. We can talk," she paused, "later." Holly continued to massage between his legs, and when she was ready, she crawled on top of him. He was looking at her with sad, questioning eyes. Holly guided him to her and pushed herself back to ensure he was completely inside. She started slow movements, back and forth. The third time she slid forward, he pulled her down to him, wrapping his arms around her. He started to move with her, slowly, softly. When he looked into her eyes, Holly only saw love. They kissed. Softly. Slowly. They moved. Softly. Slowly. Soon, she felt his body stiffen, then his release. She moved back and forth a few more times, then her release came, as well. She relaxed completely on his chest, then slid to one side and molded herself to him.

"Can we?" he started.

"No. I'll let you know when. I just want to be here, with you. Like this. For a while."

Holly had a few boyfriends over the years. She'd had sex with some. Some weren't worth it. This was different. Those men – maybe boys, were all about fast, physical sex, almost like it was a wrestling match to see who won or lost. Most didn't care what happened to her. This was different. This was an intimacy that she hadn't known. Their eyes had connected. Their kisses. The way he'd responded to her. And she realized that she had connected with him more in that short time than she ever had with Josh. So, what did that mean?

She felt his arm envelop her and pull her closer. Even more than during sex, she felt like she was one with him. She closed her eyes and drifted off.

When Holly woke, they were still together in the sleeping bag. She nuzzled into Pete as if she were a cat and made a purring sound.

"So, I take it we can talk now?" he asked.

"Yes. As long as you don't make it too intellectual, or something sad or upsetting."

"Well, we probably ought to talk about what just happened – or what happened earlier."

"You mean the part where you took advantage of poor little innocent me?"

Pete kissed her on the forehead and said, "Yeah, that part."

"You know, if you were one of the few – and I do mean few – guys with whom I . . ." she searched for the right word.

"Got it," Pete said.

"Thank you. Anyway, I'd probably give you some answer about what a hunk you are."

"Well, that obviously won't work with me."

Holly playfully slapped his chest. "I'm not sure it wouldn't, BUT, I feel closer to you than anyone I've ever known. You care about me. You listen to me. You don't judge me. And you know what else?"

"What?" he asked.

"Right now, you're worried about me. Not what I might do or say, but about how I feel. About whether I've made a mistake. Tell me I'm wrong."

"You are, well, almost engaged, and I am old enough, most likely, to . . ."

"Stop!" she interrupted. "I don't give a rat's patootie about a number assigned because of the year you were born. And, you're in better shape, with less flab than most of the guys I dated – including Josh. Well, there were some in better shape, but they wore jock straps to school and had double digit IQs. Well, one I'm giving a break. He may actually have had an IQ in the single digits. Point is, I have no idea if or where WE are going after this, but I have to tell you I love you. There. I said it. Usually it makes guys run away. Run into the woods, if you like."

"It's my tent. Why should I run away?" He was smiling and kissed her softly.

Holly kissed him back, then said, "I hate to break the mood, but I need to use the convenience. I'm going to have to slide out of the sleeping bag to get dressed. I don't want you looking. So, turn away."

Holly slid out of the sleeping bag. It took a minute to find her things and slide them on for the cold trip to the latrine. Pete watched her the entire time. She looked tiny and vulnerable. She was also darling and beautiful. She had beautiful long red hair. Peaches and cream skin that was dotted here and there with freckles. He thought about kissing each and every one, then chided himself for the feelings he had for this young woman who was practically promised.

When she turned around, finally dressed, Pete was supporting himself on one arm, his hand under the side of his head. He was watching her intently. He had a very slight smile. His eyes gave him away.

"You cheated," she said. "You weren't supposed to look."

"Not look at a goddess? Someone once told me that if I were to gaze on someone as beautiful as you, I'd turn to stone. I think it's happening. It starts in the middle, just below the waist."

"Goddess? You're kidding, right? And what's that look on your face?"

"Worship."

"What am I going to do with you?" she said as she slipped through the tent flap to the convenience.

When she returned, Pete was dressed and putting a few more sticks on the small fire.

"No fair. You peeked. I didn't get to."

Pete smiled, kissed the top of her head, said "My turn," and slipped through the tent flap.

Fifteen

Pete returned from the convenience and put a pot of water over the fire. When the water was boiling, he added bouillon cubes. In a few minutes, he and Holly were sipping bouillon from enamel mugs.

"We still need to talk, you know," he said.

"Because we had unprotected sex and now I just might be carrying your baby?"

Pete choked on his bouillon. A little spurted out his nose. "You what?!"

"Just kidding, I'm on the pill. Serves you right, though, for peeking while a lady dresses." Holly was laughing. Then, so was Pete.

"You could have stopped my heart. Then where would you be?"

"Well, the way you reacted after I thawed you out, I could probably figure out some way to get you going again." Again, they were laughing.

Pete put more sticks on the fire and started to get things ready for breakfast.

Breakfast was again bacon and eggs, with toast as a follow-up. Pete made coffee for himself and tea for Holly. After breakfast, Pete cleaned up the dishes.

When things were put away, he turned to Holly and said, "We have to think about getting you back to civilization."

Holly looked at the ground then back up at him. "I want one more night."

"What?"

"One more night. Then, I'll go peacefully. I'm not ready to go yet."

"In spite of the bad food, the bears, and the cold toilet?"

"The food is good. You'll protect me from the bears, but you're right, the toilet needs some warmth. Still. Two out of three. I want one more night. Okay?"

"Fine with me," he was smiling, "but how are you going to explain this to everybody else?"

"Are you kidding? We've just come through a HUGE snowstorm. We couldn't take a chance on getting lost and frozen in the woods. I'm the only one who does that."

"Well, not the only one. Every year we lose at least a half dozen."

"So, one more night. You can get rid of me tomorrow."

"Get rid of you isn't the way I'd put it, but you have other places you need to be."

"And, it would seem to be shower and shampoo day," Holly said. "You wouldn't deny a girl her spa treatment, would you?"

Pete got the pot to heat water in. He put the stand around the fire to support it, then added water. He turned around to get the sleeping bag to use as a curtain. When he turned back, Holly was removing her shirt.

"Wait! Let me get this in place first," he said.

"Why?" Holly asked. She just stood waiting for an answer. When Pete had none, she said, "I thought so. No reason. So, come over here and help me. I didn't get a proper wash down on Wednesday. You can help me get one now." She started undoing her jeans.

Pete was trying to say something, but nothing coherent would come out of his mouth.

"Well, come here."

Pete slowly walked over to her. She was removing her jeans, then her briefs. "Here," she said handing them to him. "Put those over there." He placed them where she had indicated then returned to her. His legs were shaking. "Thank you. And, thank you for coming back. I'd hate to have to tell you where I want you all the time. Shows you can be trained." She smiled and kissed him.

"Now, you might as well get out of your clothes. We don't want them to get wet while you wash me. And, then I can wash you, too."

"Look," he started, "I'm really not sure . . ."

Holly stepped very close to him. "Later. We can talk later. A very wise man, who saved my life, by the way, and that makes him important, too, but as I was saying, a very wise man once told me to do the important things now. The unimportant things, like talking about it, can wait until later. That's what later is for – the unimportant things." By this time, Holly had his belt undone and was unbuttoning his trousers.

"I was just going to say that I'm not sure that this is the . . ."

Holly was pushing his trousers and underwear down. His erection was growing. "Well, SOMEBODY apparently thinks it is a good idea," she said.

"That part really doesn't think," said Pete. "And to be truthful, when Little Pete is getting his way, the rest of the intellect shuts down completely."

"Well that's good," said Holly. "Just follow my direction and everything will be fine." She finished removing his trousers and pulled off his sweater. They were now naked, standing inches apart. She wetted a wash cloth and put some soap on it. "Here. Wash my back – please."

Pete started to turn her around, but she shook her head and stepped closer to him. Their bodies were now touching. "It will be warmer this way. Just reach around me." She pulled her hair out of the way. Pete took the cloth and reached around Holly. He had to pull her tight against himself in order to do the washing. He wasn't sure if he was in heaven or hell. Heaven was the feeling running through him. Heaven was the joy he felt. Hell was the thought that he shouldn't be doing this.

Holly directed him in what he thought was excruciating detail about how she wanted to be washed. Back progressed to shoulders, and arms, then her derriere and legs. She made him wash her derriere without the cloth – with his bare hands, asking all the time if he thought she had a cute tush or if it was too big, too soft, too anything. Then, she wanted everything in front washed. Slowly and carefully. He thought she was delighting in his discomfort. If she was, she delighted even more when she started to wash him. She took special care on his most delicate and intimate areas.

Finally, the washing, rinsing, and drying were done. He started to turn for his clothes. "What are you doing?" Holly asked.

"I'm – I thought – we were . . ."

"You already told me that when Little Pete was in charge you needed direction to get anything done." She took him by the hand. "So, follow me." Pete hesitated. Holly let go of his hand and wrapped her hand around his erection. "So, now follow me." She led him to the sleeping bag and pulled him down onto it. "So, here's the thing," she started. "Over the next hour – maybe two, I plan to explore every inch of your body and make this an afternoon you'll remember for the rest of your life. I hope – I'm asking you to do the same for me."

Sixteen

Two hours later, Pete and Holly fell asleep in each other's arms. They didn't sleep long, but they slept well. They awoke after about two hours. The sun was starting its downward run to sunset.

Holly snuggled against Pete. She kissed his chest and said, "There, that wasn't so bad, was it?"

"No. Actually, it was wonderful. And, I probably will remember that for the rest of my life." Then, after a pause, "But we really should talk."

"About what?" Holly asked. "I already told you that I love you. I don't say that lightly. And, it isn't just because you saved my life, although that counts. And I know you don't say it lightly. But men are so simple. I can read it in your eyes. I saw it in your eyes the other day. So, even if you don't say it – for whatever reason, I know it is true."

"Yes, it is true. I do love you. But your destiny lies elsewhere. Not here. Not with me."

"One thing I've learned in my twenty-nine years is that life has a way of turning what's supposed to be on its head."

"Yeah, well tomorrow morning, we're going to walk you out to civilization. And, we'll probably never see each other again. Yes. I love you. And as much as I know it will hurt, tomorrow I've got to return you to where you belong."

Pete slipped out of the sleeping bag, kissed Holly, and started getting into his clothes. "I've got to go to the store for dinner," he said. He donned his jacket and headed out of the tent. Holly sat staring at the tent, trying to sort out her

thoughts. But her thoughts were like pool balls on the break –
a whole lot of them, all going in different directions.

Dinner was subdued. Pete fixed a steak. There wasn't a
lot. Pete explained that he only brought one steak, and they
would have to share. Holly told him that he should have it
himself. She didn't want him to starve. He laughed. He said
he'd rather go without than not share.

Cleanup after dinner went quickly, and soon it was time
to head for bed. Pete put extra sticks for the fire within easy
reach. Each made their last convenience visit, then crawled
into the sleeping bag. Holly asked Pete to cocoon her. She
said it made her feel safe, which it did. But she just wanted to
be near him. He wrapped his arms around her and pulled her
close. She was safe, secure, and in heaven. She was also
incredibly sad to know this was ending tomorrow. She tried
not to let him know she was crying. She didn't know he was
doing the same thing.

Seventeen

Saturday morning came too fast. Pete and Holly tried to stall in bed as long as they could, but eventually, they had to admit defeat. Pete used the convenience first, and when Holly got there, she found the candles burning. Four candles. It was almost balmy.

Breakfast was cooked and the dishes cleaned. Holly knew she would miss watching Pete cooking simple meals over the camp fire. Before long, they were getting ready to head out.

"It's about fifteen miles to the nearest point in civilization. We'll head that way. We should be there in five or six hours."

"But then, you have five or six hours back. It will be dark by then. You should come with me."

"In many ways, I'd love to, but then there will be TV cameras, interviews, all that stuff I don't want or need. In fact, you might just tell them all you know is my first name. We were hunkered down so tight in the storm that we didn't have much time for anything but survival."

"But you deserve recognition – thanks."

"The only thanks that will ever matter is yours, and I know I have that. Everything they would say is trivial when compared to your thanks." Pete rummaged around in a pack. He pulled out a wooden box. When he opened it, there was another box inside.

"You know, you are right. Life can be funny. You never know how things will work out, or if they will. I bought this for my wife – ordered it before, well, before I lost her."

"No." Holly said. "I couldn't . . ."

"Listen. I ordered a rose, inset with emeralds. A pendant. It was delivered after – after, you know."

Both Holly and Pete looked at the ground for a minute.

"I didn't open it for a year. Forgot about it actually. When I did, I found the order had gotten messed up. They didn't send a rose at all. But, I decided to carry it with me. I never thought I'd give it to anyone."

"No. Really. I can't."

"But, funny thing, this is what they sent." Pete picked up the gold chain and pulled the pendant out of the box. It was a perfectly rendered holly leaf, set with emeralds. "I guess the universe is trying to tell me who to give it to."

Holly was gasping for air. The pendant was so beautiful she couldn't believe it. AND, it was a holly leaf. "Oh, no. I can't. It's too beautiful and it has meaning for you."

"I told you. A mistake in the order. After – after the fact."

"I guess I shouldn't tell you that Holly wasn't my parents first choice for my name. Only someone my mom didn't like took the one meant for me. So, I ended up Holly. In case you are wondering, the other name, the one I was supposed to get – was Rose. I guess two things were supposed to be Rose – and turned out to be Holly. What are the odds?"

"I'd say they were actually pretty good – now."

They kissed. Pete had Holly put on the mukluks to keep her feet warm and dry on their trek, and they headed out.

"How will you know how to get there?" asked Holly.

Pete with mock self-importance said, "This is a compass. And this is a map. As anyone can tell you, they are indispensable in getting around in the forest. Even on a day hike."

Holly slapped his arm. "Anyone can tell you NOW." And they both laughed.

Going was slow at times. Pete helped her every time she needed it and was patient beyond belief. Holly had been on hikes with others, even Josh, who were constantly complaining about her holding the group up. Pete was the perfect gentleman helping her every time she looked like she was struggling. He answered all her questions patiently.

About six hours after they left the camp, Pete slowed. Holly went to his side. Down the slope in front of them was a parking area. Snow had been plowed out. Two police cars and four other cars were parked in the lot. A group was huddled between the cars.

"There you go. Down the slope and back into life."

"I've finally seen life. I hate to leave."

"I hate for you to leave, but it is your place. But I'll never forget you Holly Franklin. You touched my heart and you touched my soul."

They kissed. Holly started down the slope. She had a tear in her eye. Halfway down the slope, she turned to wave. Pete waved back. Holly couldn't see the tears in his eyes.

Holly got to the parking area. She turned, but there was only a vacant spot where Pete had been standing. She turned back, walked to one of the officers and said, "Hi. My name is Holly Franklin. I've been lost in the forest for a few days. Could someone give me a ride?"

The trooper turned and asked, "Holly Franklin? We've been out searching for you all day. Are you okay?" Then, he yelled, "Hey! She's here. Safe!" And a great cheer went up from the entire group. Holly was left wondering what the big deal was.

Eighteen

In the KLMN television studio in Denver, the lights came on. The anchor took his seat. His assistant took a quick look to make sure everything was in its place. He looked at the camera, and the director held up five fingers, which he used to count down to when the broadcast would go 'live.' The station's news bulletin music played in the background.

"Good afternoon. This is Bob Jenkins in the KLMN news room with a news bulletin for all those in the Denver and western Colorado areas. The young woman feared lost in the Roosevelt National Forest has been found safe. Holly Franklin walked out of the woods some thirty miles from where her car was found yesterday morning. Although details are sketchy at this time, it appears Miss Franklin survived after she wandered into a camp that had been set up earlier. She was admitted to Poudre Valley Memorial Hospital for observation. As more information becomes available we will have it here for you first."

Nineteen

Holly sat in her reclined bed in a private room in the hospital. Reporters had been clamoring for interviews, but the staff had managed to keep them at bay. Her dinner sat on the tray. She had picked at it, but she wasn't really hungry. The only thing she had done that she'd enjoyed was use a 'convenience' in a warm room and take a hot shower. The shower was heavenly, but somehow, she would have preferred another sponge bath with Pete.

The nurse came into the room and announced that Holly had a visitor, if she wished. The visitor's name was Joshua Reynolds. Holly told the nurse it would be fine.

Josh entered the room with a big smile on his face. "There's my girl. I knew you'd be okay."

"Hi, Josh."

"You doing okay? You look a little down."

"Well, there was the whole lost in the forest for four days thing going on. I was lucky to stumble on that campsite. Actually, I didn't stumble on it. The camper heard me yell and he found me. Otherwise, I'd be . . ."

Josh cut her off. "I was worried. I was barely able to concentrate at the meeting this week."

"Meeting?"

"Yeah. The meeting about compliance – the one in St. Louis. Wednesday through Friday."

"Wasn't that meeting optional?"

"Yeah, but I figure it will give me a leg up. You know, for our future. It'll help get me the promotions so we can do all kinds of things later. And get us a better house down the road."

"So, I was missing. In a forest. During a snowstorm. And you went to St. Louis for a meeting you really didn't have to attend?"

"Well, when you say it like that, it sounds like I don't care. But this will be important, you know, for later, and it isn't like I could have helped out anyway."

"You're right, Josh." Holly pressed the call button. The nurse arrived in less than a minute. "I'm feeling tired. I need to sleep. Could you escort Mr. Reynolds out, please? Thanks for coming, Josh. I know it was a long drive and you have work tomorrow."

"Yeah. Right. Will you be at work on Monday?" Josh said the last as the nurse hauled him from the room.

The nurse returned. "You okay, honey? I hope that guy isn't somebody special. He's kind of a jerk."

The nurse turned off the lights. Holly could see the mountains and wondered how Pete was doing. And where he was. She was tired. But it was a different kind of tired. She lay awake, staring at the ceiling, thinking about the last four days – and the rest of her life.

Twenty

Just past midnight, Pete had returned to his camp. The fire was out in the fire ring, so he restarted that. He reset the line around the camp with the jingle bell warning system. He used the convenience and headed to bed.

The sleeping bag felt big. Bigger than usual. There was the lingering fragrance of Holly in it, as well. Despite more than ten hours of hiking, he lay awake for a long time. He might have to get rid of the sleeping bag. Too many memories. And, as soon as he could reasonably break camp, he'd do so. Maybe head over to Red Feather Lakes, like he'd planned. Ever since his wife had passed, camping had given him a place of solitude. A place to get away from it all. Now, there was a sense of loneliness associated with the camp. If he couldn't regain his solitude, if this feeling of loss persisted, he'd do away with camping altogether.

Holly left the hospital on Sunday afternoon, having been pronounced fit and well by the staff. They said they were amazed she was in such good shape after her ordeal. She stayed away from work on Monday and Tuesday, feigning fatigue and general malaise. The bank manager said he understood. Josh sent twenty texts, mostly encouraging her to return to work as soon as possible because if her work piled up, promotions might be given to others.

At night, Holly spent her time on the internet, looking up information about camping spots in Colorado. And, places to buy camping gear. A week after her return, Holly headed to a camping outlet to see about buying some things. When she left the store, she'd spent about a thousand dollars. She figured Josh would be mad; she'd spent money reserved for 'later,' but then, it actually was her money. She'd purchased a good parka with an insulated hood. She picked out what was called an elephant's foot, a half sleeping bag that covered the legs and made the good parka into a warm sleeping bag. She got a decent pack, sweater, trousers, a tarp to make a lean-to or pup tent if needed. For that, she purchased line and a hatchet. She got a first aid kit, and a good compass and maps of the area. Then, she got a book and read up on the compass and maps. Her most expensive purchase was a pair of good boots, already broken in.

Holly went to her manager and told him there had been a family emergency. She would need to use a week of vacation time in order to take care of things. The manager was sympathetic and granted the time. He said he hoped everything would work out okay. As Holly left the bank he watched. He thought she'd had a tough go the last few weeks and wished her well.

Twenty-one

Dear Josh,

I'm sorry to do this via a note, but daylight is burning, and I've got somewhere to be. I've come to realize that we want very different things out of life. Those things are not compatible, and I don't believe we are, either. I wish you well and hope you find what it is you are looking for.

Always,

Holly

Twenty-two

Stanley Ranger, with the forest service, watched the four-year-old Toyota Corolla turn off the two-lane asphalt road and into the parking lot. The car came to a stop twenty feet away, close to the log parking barrier. The driver got out of the car. The ranger saw it was a young woman. She seemed to be dressed for hiking and camping, but he also saw the things she seemed to be wearing and packing were all new. He was skeptical about a newbie going off into the forest alone.

The woman walked to the office holding a map and read the ranger's name tag. "Ranger Ranger?" she asked with a smile.

"Don't start," he replied. "With a last name like Ranger, what else could I do? At least my parents didn't name me Rick. How can I help you?"

"I'm trying to meet up with someone here in the area, but I'm not sure exactly where he'll be. He said something about the north west side of the lakes. That would be here – right?" Holly pointed to the place on the map where she thought Pete was likely to camp.

"That's the general area, yes. Kind of a large area. Do you have any information that would narrow it down?"

"Well, I have an idea that he's looking for some solitude, so he probably won't be around any large gatherings or facilities."

"That would put him – probably – in this area," he said pointing to a place on her map. "Mind if I draw it in?"

"No. Please. Any help is appreciated."

The ranger drew a circle around an area. "I know you won't think it is any part of my business, but the things you have are all new. The area you're going to is pretty remote. Do you know what you're doing – camping-wise, that is? I'm asking because if you happen to get into trouble, we'll have to come search for you."

Holly was studying the map. "No problem." She took his pencil and drew a line on the map. "I'm planning to hike along this route up to the area you showed me. I don't plan to be gone for more than five days. I'll check back in here when I return. Okay?"

"Better than most. Thank you. Would you fill out an information card for me – just in case?"

"Sure. No problem."

Holly filled out the card and handed it to the ranger. "Holly Franklin. That name seems familiar. Do I know you?"

"I don't think so. Probably a common name."

Holly returned to her car and put her pack on her back, adjusting the pack frame. She started off into the woods.

"Good luck finding . . ." the ranger shouted.

Holly waved and said loud enough for no one to hear, "a name."

Twenty-three

Six hours later, Holly was getting close to the area she wanted to search. But, it was getting dark, and she decided to stop for the night. She found a clearing and dropped her pack from her back. It would have been a difficult load, but the pack frame made carrying it much easier than it would have been. She took the tarp she had packed and aluminum poles that made a small A frame. She put the rope over the poles and fixed it into the ground using tent pegs. Then, she draped the tarp over the rope and poles making a small tent. She fastened the edges of the tent into the ground. Into her makeshift tent, she put the elephant's foot. Dinner was a sandwich. She wanted more, but she'd decided to take it easy, especially on this first night. She might need to conserve food. She found a tree about ten yards away and used another piece of rope to hoist her food about fifteen feet off the ground, as Pete had done.

Holly crawled into the tent and blocked the entrance, more or less, with her pack. She thought about Pete's camp. Compared to her accommodations now, his teepee was like a five-star hotel. She slid her legs into the elephant's foot, used some extra clothing for a pillow, and, worn out by her hike in the forest, drifted off to sleep. She dreamt about the nights she'd spent with Pete and what it was like to have him wrapped around her.

Five miles away, Pete was bedding down for the night. He lay awake staring at the inside of the tent, remembering the young woman who had invaded his solitude. He was glad he had found her. His mind rejected the thoughts of what would have happened to her if he hadn't heard her cry for help. It would have been a young life wasted. He wondered where she was and what she was doing. Then, thoughts wandered to the way she had basically taken over his life. He smiled. He'd decided that he had very much enjoyed having her take over. Eventually, he fell asleep and dreamt of wrapping himself around her.

Holly woke as the sun started to rise. She felt stiff and sore. She appreciated the blankets Pete had put on the teepee floor. And whatever he'd put under the sleeping bag to make it feel more like a bed. She unfastened the elephant's foot, moved her pack, and crawled out of the tent. She thought, *I wish Pete were here to make coffee. It was nice to have it ready when I crawled out of bed.* Then, she thought, *change that. I just wish Pete were here.* She'd packed dehydrated food, so she heated some water on a sterno stove she'd brought and used it to make both the breakfast and some coffee. She didn't want to waste the water. She needed it and it was heavy. She had purification filters and kits in case she found a stream, but she was hoping she wouldn't have to resort to that.

Holly packed up after breakfast. Lunch would be an MRE. Maybe dinner, too. She'd planned out her strategy. She looked at her map and decided to look in the far corner of the park first. It would take most of the day. She'd try to find a better spot to camp, but she realized that the very act of moving the entire day would mean she would have to take the best of what there was when it was time to stop for the day. Holly donned her pack and adjusted it. She looked at the map and checked her compass, then headed out.

By the end of the day, Holly had covered the area she'd wanted to. She had to push, and she was tired, but she was happy that she had accomplished what she had planned. Almost better, and something she was most proud of, was that she knew where she was. She wasn't lost. Nobody was going to have to search for her. Then, she thought about managing her time. This was the end of her first day. She had four more. If she didn't find Pete by the end of the fourth day, she'd have to use the fifth to return to the ranger station. If she caused two searches in the period of a month she was sure she would be a pariah in the eyes of emergency crews everywhere.

Holly made camp and had an MRE for her evening meal. They were incredibly high in calories, but she figured she was burning them up pretty fast wandering around in the wilderness. She also made a fire using the small, portable camp heater she'd bought. She'd been cold last night, and despite the warmth generated by her activity, she felt the temperature dropping. The heater was a godsend. She prepared for the night the same way she had the previous night. She decided to change her plans for the next day. The highest point in the area wasn't far from where she was. She thought if she could get to the highest ground, she might just be able to see the top of the teepee she hoped Pete was still using. She climbed into the elephant's foot, arranged her pack in front of the tent opening, and closed her eyes to sleep.

Holly's sleep was fitful. She had a dream about coming to the end of the trail and nothing was there. Literally nothing. There was the end of the trail and then nothing. When she turned around, the road back was disappearing, as well. She awoke in a sweat. *What if there is nothing ahead for me? I can't go back.* She lay awake for some time. Finally, she noticed the sky was getting lighter in the East. Tired from lack of sleep and fatigued from her ordeal, she roused herself. She didn't have the motivation to fix a hot breakfast. She realized that it was only the second day and thought that if she was too tired to fix meals, it might be a problem. She grabbed an MRE and ate it as fast as she could. She packed up and lifted the pack to her back. She wanted to get to the high ground. She had great hope for that. She didn't want to think about getting up there and not finding anything. The thought of going back without finding Pete was too depressing to linger on.

She checked her map and compass, then looked at the direction she would be heading. Uphill okay. If nothing else, she was happy she knew where she was and where she was going. As she started out, she hoped it would be the same in her life.

Twenty-four

Pete stoked the fire he'd made outside his tent. He preferred cooking – and being – outside when the weather permitted. It had been a cold night, but the sun was up, and the day warming. He retrieved some bacon and eggs from his cold storage. Then, he realized that he had gotten out too much food. *She was only with me for four days*, he thought. *How could she have affected me so deeply?* Actually, he knew quite well, it was just that he didn't want to admit it because he knew he'd never see her again.

Pete scrambled the eggs and added them to the already cooked bacon. He grilled some bread and buttered the resulting toast. As always, the food cooked in the wild had a specialness all its own. But there was something else. A sadness he hadn't had to contend with previously. He knew what it was. He thought he'd have to stop camping if the sense of loss continued. Take up something else. Sailing, maybe. He didn't know.

He took his time cleaning up. He straightened the camp and, because the weather was good, took the opportunity to shower outdoors – warm water poured through a can with holes poked in the bottom serving as the shower. Then, he shaved and dressed. He decided to have a cup of tea and heated water. Then, he sat down next to the fire in a low camp chair. The morning was quiet. He tried to immerse himself in the day.

Pete looked down the long hill leading up to his camp. He thought he'd seen movement. Although he scanned from

side to side, he concentrated mostly on the place where he thought he'd seen something move. He was out in the back woods, and things happened out here. Occasionally, bad things. He kept a pistol, smaller than his Ruger, in the event that someone wanted to do him harm. He got it and put it into a bag beside the chair.

Sure enough, there was movement down the hill, coming his way. He sipped his tea. As the figure came closer, he could see it had to be a hiker, a good-sized pack on his back. A big floppy hat covered the face. He was moving along slowly, but steadily. Closer the figure came. The hiker appeared to be rather small, maybe not even five feet six. Pete wondered whether it could be a woman. *What would a woman be doing out here by herself? If she is by herself.* Pete didn't relax his guard. Then, he saw a flash. On the hiker's chest. Gold and green. At first, it didn't register, but then, slowly his mind started to wonder if the impossible was indeed possible.

Holly walked into the clearing and saw Pete sitting by the fire. He wasn't moving. Maybe he was in shock. The thought made her smile. She walked up to the fire and dropped her pack. She nodded toward his tea. As if in a trance, he handed it to her. She took a good mouthful. It tasted like heaven. *Earl Grey*, she thought, *with a touch of sweetness.* She reminded herself to remember that.

Pete stood. Holly looked at him. A tear ran down his cheek. Holly said, "We have to talk." Then, she took him by the hand. And said, "Later." And she led him into the tent and closed the flap.

Epilog

It took Josh Reynolds almost a week to get over losing Holly. One of the bank's tellers, a pretty blonde with limited intelligence and large assets, caught his eye. They were married in two months, at her insistence. He had no way of knowing that she would run up his debts into six figures before leaving him for someone else.

Holly and Pete stayed on the mountain for another day before heading back to the ranger station to announce they were safe. They were married two months later. Holly quit her job and does consulting on financial matters. Pete decided to stop his camping adventures. He says he's no longer trying to get away from anything. He has everything he needs. They live in Pete's four-bedroom house. One is their bedroom. One is their office. They also have a guest room, but the fourth is being converted. Holly and Pete's first child will arrive in three months. If Holly has any complaint it is that Pete pays almost too much attention to her.

Thank you for reading my book. I hope you enjoyed it.

If you enjoyed this book, please leave a review. Reviews help other readers find books they would like to read and help authors improve their own works.

In addition, if you would like to be one of my beta reviewers – someone who reads my books before publication and who receives the completed book free of charge, please send your name and e-mail address to my publisher at TWeaver2008@aol.com to be included in this group. You may opt out at any time.

BOOKS by Anna Leigh

Loves Lost & Found – A Mystery Romance Adventure

Lost in the Forest – A Romantic Wilderness Adventure

.

Anna Leigh

ABOUT THE AUTHOR

Anna Leigh lives in suburban Maryland. She enjoys musical theater, loves to travel, and cares for small animals. She also enjoys fitness activities and has completed numerous Spartan challenges.

Made in the USA
Middletown, DE
08 October 2018